For Noa, Tristan and Jade

First published in the United States and Canada in 2015 by Lemniscaat USA LLC · New York
Distributed in the United States by Lemniscaat USA LLC · New York

Library of Congress Cataloging-in-Publication Data is available.
ISBN 13: 978-1-935954-46-0 (Hardcover)
Printing and binding: Worzalla, Stevens Point, WI USA
First U.S. edition

Maranke Rinck & Martijn van der Linden

The Other Rabbit

Translated by Laura Watkinson

LEMNISCAAT

Rabbit is looking for the other rabbit.

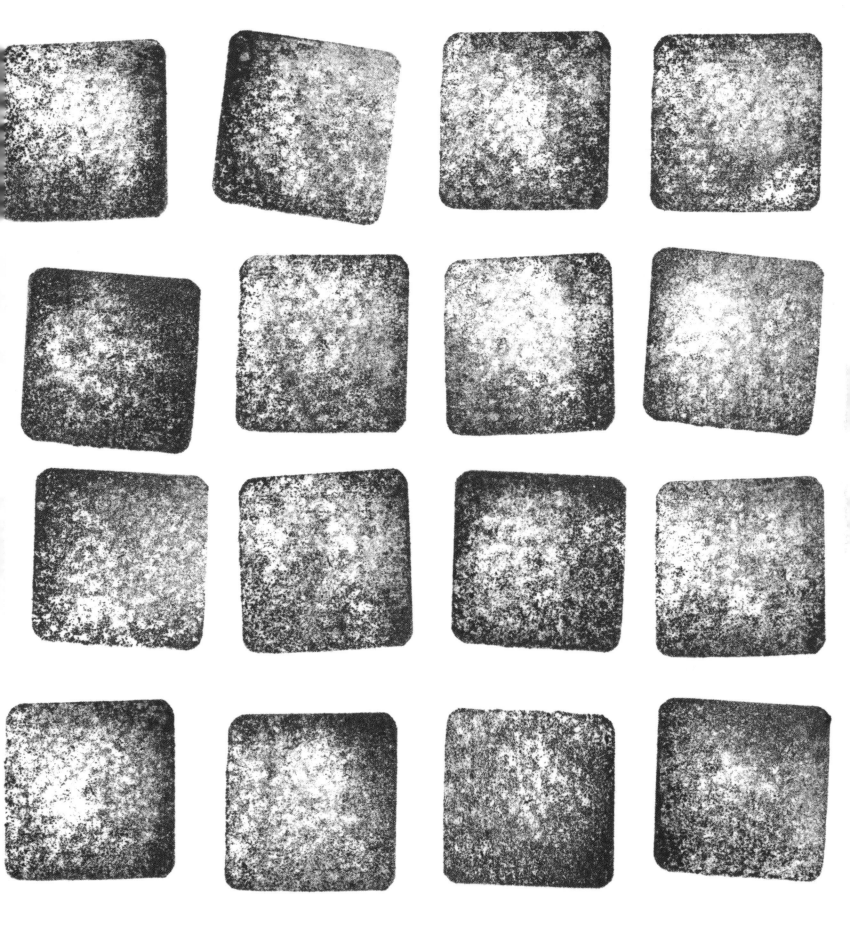

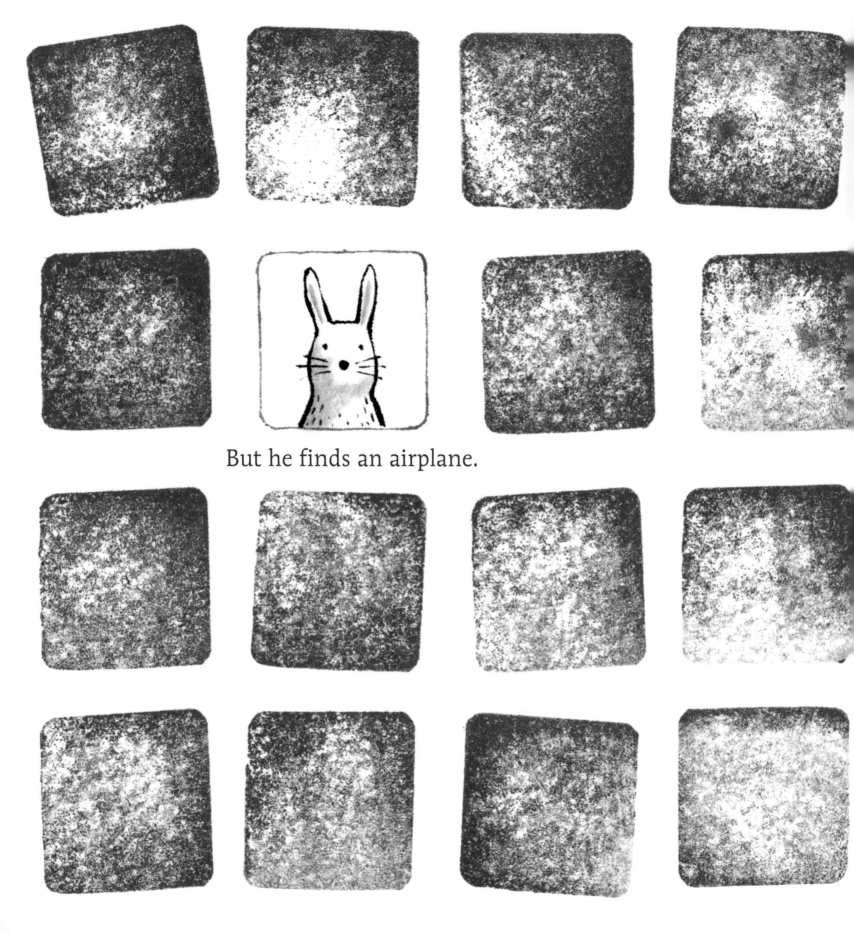

But he finds an airplane.

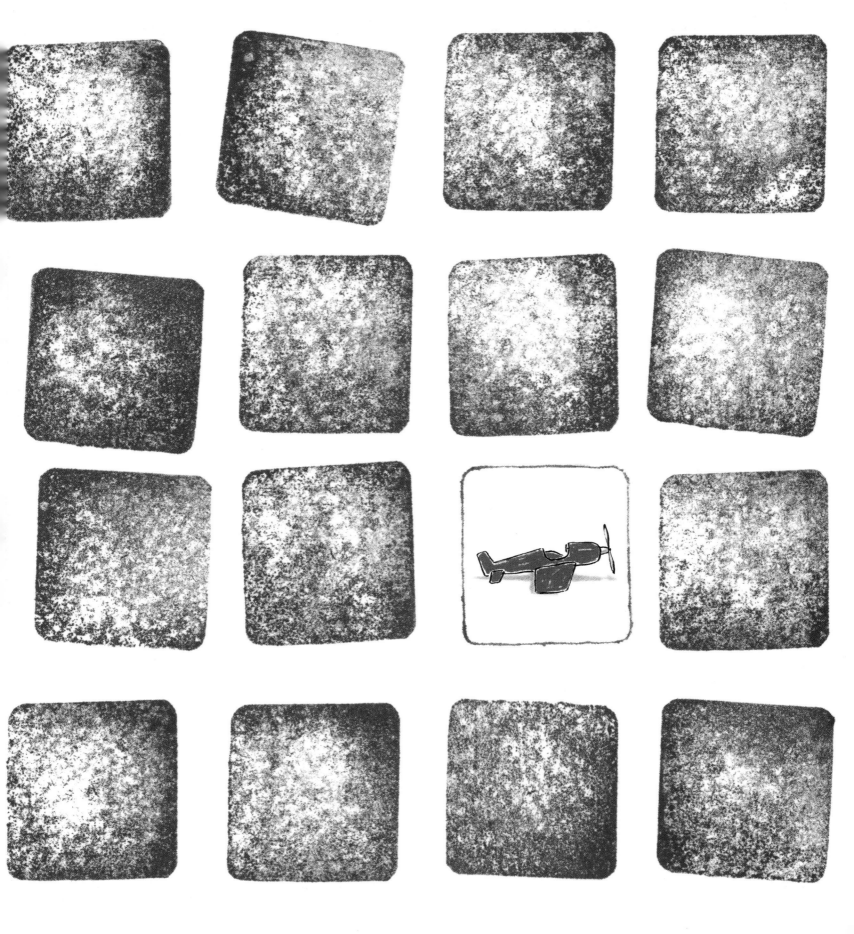

"Where's the other rabbit?"
Rabbit asks the birds.

"We don't know. Can we help you look for him?"

Some more birds come flying toward them
They're flying to the sun.
Suddenly all the birds
want to fly to the sun.

So Rabbit has to go on alone.
And now there's something wrong with his airplane!

He quickly lands on an island.

He sees another airplane.
But that one is broken, too.

Then Rabbit meets a king.
"Have you seen the other rabbit?"

"No," says the king.
"But I do know..."

The king doesn't finish his sentence,
because someone honks a horn.
Another king gets out of the car.

The kings shake hands.
They talk about kingly things.
And they forget about Rabbit.

Rabbit coughs.

"Oh, yes," says the king.

"You were looking for the other rabbit.

I'm busy right now. Ask my animal friends."

"I have an idea!" says the other king.
"You can take my car."

Rabbit races across the island.

Beeeeep!

That was almost a crash!

The chicken gets out. So does Rabbit.

"Sorry. I didn't see you," says Rabbit.
"Because I was looking for the other rabbit.
Or the king's animal friends. They might be able to help."

"The animals live over there," says the chicken.
"I'll go with you."

"The Dragon!" shout the animals.
"The other rabbit is with the dragon. She carried him away!"
"Then I will have to fight the dragon," says Rabbit.

"Hold on," say the animals. "Wait a moment..."

"There's a dragon on this island, too.
But the dragon you're looking for is on the other island."

"How do I get to the other island?" asks Rabbit.
"We're good swimmers," say the animals. "You can go on our backs."

Another bunch of animals is swimming in the sea.

The animals are all very happy to see each other.
So happy that they want to have a party.
Right now!

So Rabbit climbs into a boat.
The fish carry him some of the way.
Until they find some other fish and
all the fish swim off together.

Rabbit leaves his boat on the beach. There's the dragon!

"Do you have the other rabbit?"

"You can't have him," says the dragon.
   "Because without Rabbit I'll be all alone."
      "But I want him," says Rabbit.
The dragon shakes her head.

"Then I'm going to fight you.
And I'm going to win!" says Rabbit.
   "You can try," says the dragon.

Rabbit flew an airplane and drove a car.
He swam in the sea and sailed a boat.
But now he knows where the other rabbit is...
and they can't be together!

Then Rabbit has an idea.

Rabbit whispers
something
to the beetle.

Before long, Rabbit points up into the sky.
The dragon sees it, too. She smiles.

"Did someone send for me?" says the other dragon.
The dragon jumps into the air and the two dragons fly away.

And Rabbit is finally,
finally together with...—

... the other rabbit. That's a pair!